Praise for *Albert: A Frog and His Dream*

"*Albert: A Frog and His Dream* is one of those rare books that is both an enjoyable read and carries a valuable lesson in life. Until Albert proved differently, no frog could fly. He had a dream and the desire and fortitude to follow it, proving that dreams can come true. It's a book that will be read many times over."

—Paul Sinor, author and screenwriter

"What a wonderful story. A real 'page turner,' as they say. I liked Albert's perseverance despite the ridicule, and the story had me guessing whether he would end up failing but learning from that experience or actually succeeding and attaining his dream. I was happy he succeeded.
"I think my five-year-old grandson will enjoy this book, and his old grandpa loves its positive message. And the illustrations! Simply beautiful. They remind me of classic children's books from yesteryear."

—Paul Archipley, owner/publisher, Beacon Publishing, Mukilteo, WA

"*Albert: A Frog and His Dream* is destined to be a classic. This is a tale that children will remember into their adulthood and want to share with their own children. The story is so well written that it stays with you in your heart. It is told in such a way that children of all ages—as well as adults—will understand and appreciate its message. Unlike a lot of children's books, the author does not talk down to his audience, but rather talks to them. The illustrations are absolutely lovely and worthy of framing and displaying. I sincerely hope that there will be more adventures in Albert's future."

—Victoria Dadi, screenwriter

ALBERT

A Frog and His Dream

BELLE ISLE BOOKS
www.belleislebooks.com

Doug Warren

Illustrations by Keegan Williams

ISBN: 978-1-953021-46-5
LCCN: 2021918363

Project managed by Haley Simpkiss

Printed in the United States of America

Published by
Belle Isle Books (an imprint of Brandylane Publishers, Inc.)
5 S. 1st Street
Richmond, Virginia 23219

BELLE ISLE BOOKS
www.belleislebooks.com

belleislebooks.com | brandylanepublishers.com

For Sophie & Daphne

Albert was a tree frog.
He was like all of his tree frog friends and family in many ways,
except for one . . .

Albert was a dreamer.

Every day, Albert would go to a tall tree
near the big pond and climb as high as he
could to observe how all the other animals in the forest
spent their days. And as he observed, he would wonder:

How are deer so big
but still so quiet?

What do the fish
think about all day?

How do birds make
such beautiful music?

2

Birds were Albert's absolute
favorite animals to watch.
He loved seeing them
fly gracefully from
treetop to treetop

Albert wanted to fly
just like the birds.

Albert began to collect any feathers he could find.
One morning, he ran into Sam the salamander and a few of his friends.
"What on earth are you doing, Albert?" asked Sam.
"I'm going to make my own wings so I can fly!" Albert said.

4

"Albert," said Sam, "frogs can't fly. You know that, right?"
Then Sam laughed at Albert and said, "Oh, Albert,
why can't you just be happy being a tree frog?"
Sam and his friends doubled over laughing at Albert and his silly dream.
Albert felt a bit hurt but simply went on with his business.

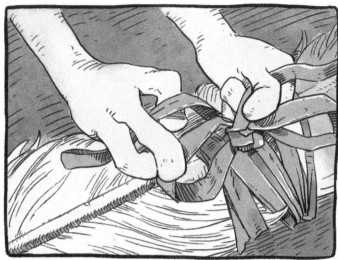

Albert was confident. He had solved a lot of difficult problems over the years, and he was not going to let his friends' laughter change his mind. "You can do whatever you want to do if you believe in yourself," Albert quipped. "All you need is a little imagination."

As the weeks wore on, Albert's friends would ask him about his wings. One of them would say, "It's such a beautiful and clear sky today. How are your wings coming along, Albert?" while the rest tried to cover up their giggles.

But Albert would just
smile and respond,
"Fine, thank you,"
and carry on working.

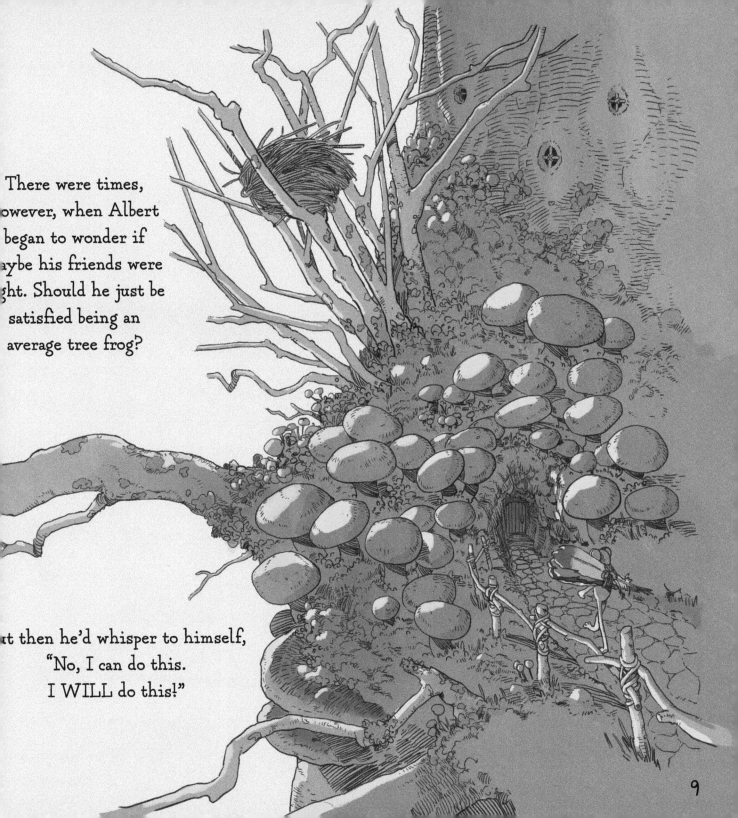

There were times, however, when Albert began to wonder if maybe his friends were right. Should he just be satisfied being an average tree frog?

But then he'd whisper to himself, "No, I can do this. I WILL do this!"

9

Albert worked tirelessly on his wings for months,
making sure he had just the right feathers set in just the right way.
Once he felt his wings were ready, he climbed the tallest tree in the forest,
tugging his wings along with him. At the very top, he slipped them on.

Albert looked down. "Maybe I am just a tree frog!" he shouted.
"But I am a tree frog who can FLY!"
The other animals in the forest stopped what they were doing to look up.
Albert felt a lump in his throat as he got to his feet. Someone shouted,
"Frogs can't fly!" and Albert could hear some of the
animals below laughing, as if he had lost his mind.

But by now, Albert was used to everyone doubting him, and he simply ignored the laughter coming up from below. Albert slowly and proudly spread his wings. Suddenly, everything became very, very quiet. The animals couldn't believe what they were seeing. Albert's wings were so beautiful. The laughter stopped. Everything stopped.

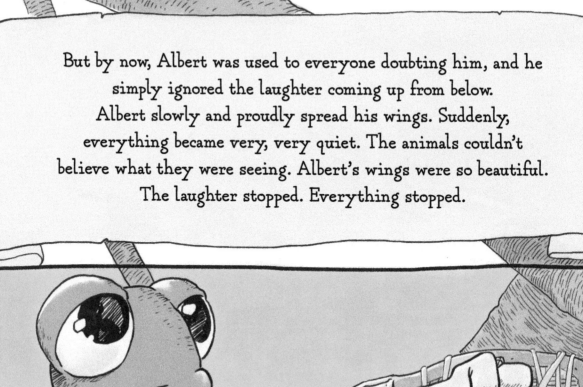

13

Albert closed his eyes and took a deep breath.
Then, he did it. He stepped off the tree branch.
He dropped quickly! Maybe too quickly, he thought, afraid that
maybe he'd made a mistake. But then an amazing thing happened.
Albert felt himself slow and begin to lift. His wings—they worked!
They worked PERFECTLY! Albert was flying—REALLY FLYING!
He flew once around the pond for everyone to see.
Albert could see the entire forest.

Albert was flying confidently, and rather fast, as he returned to land, buzzing over the crowd. Then he slowed and gently landed on a big tree, his sticky toes easily gripping the leaves. Albert sat very still for a moment, not quite believing what he had just done. Then he began to giggle, and before he knew it, he was laughing harder than he had ever laughed before.

Albert turned his head to look around at his friends behind him.
All of them had begun to cheer.
"WOOHOO! HOORAY!"
"That was AMAZING, Albert!" How did you do that?"
Albert sighed, and with a shrug of his shoulders
and a slight smile, he simply said . . .

I'm a dreamer!

The End

Are you an inventor like Albert?

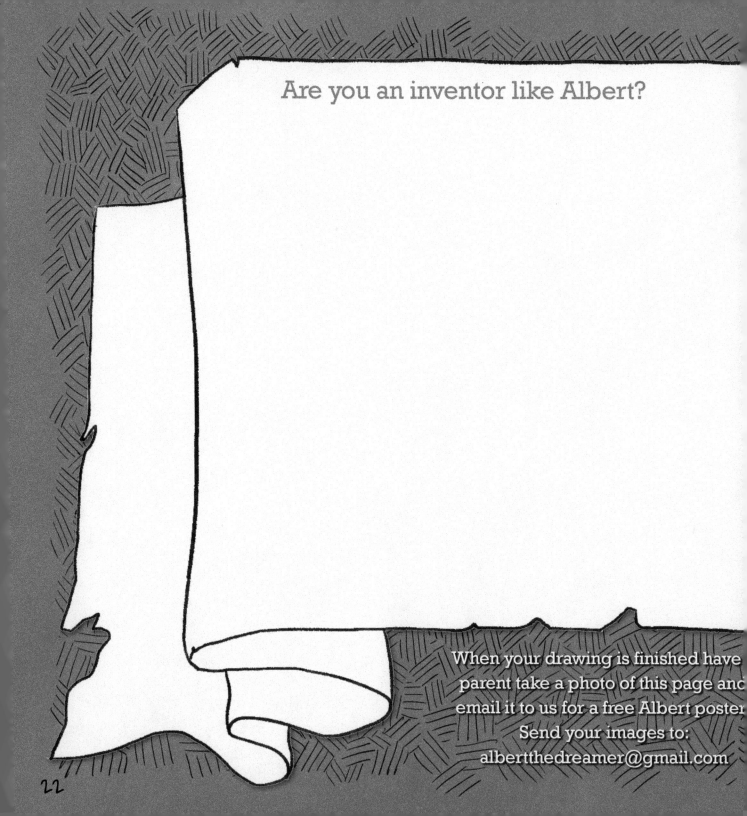

When your drawing is finished have
parent take a photo of this page and
email it to us for a free Albert poster
Send your images to:
albertthedreamer@gmail.com

22

Draw your ideas on these pages!

About the Author

Doug Warren was born in Northern California and currently lives in Lake Stevens, Washington, with his two daughters, Sophie and Daphne. A multi-faceted artist, Doug has devoted himself to teaching his two daughters to always chase their dreams, using his gifts for both music and storytelling. Doug's love of both aviation and nature are comfortably at home in the Pacific Northwest. When he's not working as a graphic artist or dreaming up new adventures for Albert, he can be found playing his original music at live shows.

About the Illustrator

Keegan Williams is an independent illustrator from western Washington. Williams began drawing at an early age, inspired by the steady diet of video games, fantasy novels, and comic books on which he was raised. These days, when not working to make rent at his day job, he enjoys channeling that initial inspiration from video games, fantasy novels, and comic books into his illustrative work.

CPSIA information can be obtained
at www.ICGtesting.com
Printed in the USA
BVHW021056210122
626778BV00002B/3